# Bibi's Gt Game

## A Story about Tennis,
## Meditation and a Dog Named Coco

### BIANCA ANDREESCU

with **Mary Beth Leatherdale**    illustrated by **Chelsea O'Byrne**

tundra

Every morning,
I wake up in a hurry.

Sometimes I pop into
my parents' room for a quick
snuggle. And to give Coco
a scritch on the head.

But I can't stay long.

Before school, I have to practice my
cartwheels. I can do 12 in a row.
The world record is 1,321.

Then I do my
backwards running.
I need to beat the
100 meters record —
13.6 seconds.

While I'm eating breakfast,
I work on balancing a spoon on my nose.
The world record is
38 minutes, 42.57 seconds.

And every single morning, Mom and Dad and Coco cheer me on.

"Dream big, win big, Bibi," Mom says.

I'm looking for some new challenges,
so Mom signs me up for a bunch of sports.

I try to like each one.
I really do.

But nothing feels quite right.

So I tell Mom I'm going back to my old workout.

One day, when I'm on my 14th cartwheel,
Dad shouts, "Bibi, come quick!"

It's the final match of the US Open tennis tournament.
After battling injuries all season, Dad's favorite player,
Kim Clijsters, is just one point away from becoming the champion!

When Kim wins the match, the crowd goes wild. So do we!

"Bibi, maybe you should try tennis," Dad says.

Tennis looks like fun. So I say, YES!

As soon as I hold the racquet in my hand,
I know this game is different.

I love being on the court. Just me and the fuzzy ball.

My coach says I'm a natural. Strong and powerful.
That tennis is my sport.

Coco hopes he's right. She loves tennis too.

I practice for hours and hours and hours.
My coach says I'm doing great.

I have a lightning-fast serve.

My backhand booms like thunder.

Best of all, my forehand is
as fierce and unpredictable
as a hurricane.

But I want to be the best, so I work on:
My stance. *Crouch low, ready to blast the ball.*

My grip. *Position my hand perfectly
to battle every shot.*

My follow-through.
*Swing strong for maximum force.*

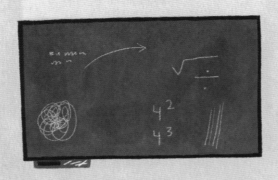

While my game gets better and better, things at school
get worse and worse.

I'm so busy with tennis that I don't have time for anything else.
No playdates. No birthday parties. No sleepovers.

When I have to leave school early for practice or a tournament,
I try to sneak out of the classroom. But someone always
notices my giant tennis bag.

She thinks she's so great.

She'll never make it in tennis.

She's just weird.

The only thing I like about school is recess.
I love swinging on the monkey bars.
My arms are super strong.

But one day, my hand slips from the bar —

# THUD!

My ankle is on fire.

A boy in my class spots me.
"Guess you won't be winning any
tennis games now!"

Until my ankle heals, I can't play tennis!
I can't do anything.

What if that boy is right?

What if I NEVER
win a tennis game
AGAIN?!

Feeling gloomy, I hide out with
Coco in our tree fort.
Coco thinks about all the best things about tennis.
I think about the worst.

When Mom finds us, I tell her I've made my decision.
"I'm quitting tennis!"

"Bibi, why rush?" Mom says. "Slow down and let your body heal.
Use this time to exercise your mind."

Mom loves to meditate. She says that it helps her to
calm her mind. And she won't leave until I try her
favorite breathing exercise.

Sitting cross-legged, our hands relaxed with palms facing up,
we close our eyes and take a few deep breaths.
Mom's words flow over us like water.

"Breathe in through your nose: 1, 2, 3, 4.
Hold the breath in: 1, 2, 3, 4.

"Breathe out through your nose: 1, 2, 3, 4.
Hold the breath outside: 1, 2, 3, 4.
And again . . . "

I try breathing slowly. I really do. But sitting and breathing is much harder than it looks.

My mind is whirling.

you'll never make it in tennis

you think you're so great

I tell Mom I'm quitting meditation too.

you're just
WEIRD

But Mom doesn't
give up so easily.

She says that meditation is a bit like magic.
Like a rabbit in a hat, there are peaceful thoughts
hidden in my mind. I just have to dig
deep to find them.

"Picture all the things that make you happy, Bibi.
All the things that you're grateful for."

I close my eyes and see:

Mom's mac and cheese

The rescue dogs we met
when we visited family in Romania

*Never Say Never* —
the best movie ever!

Coco closes her eyes too.

I feel my body relax. I notice the warmth of the sun on my strong arms. The cool breeze on my face. The *chirp, chirp, chirp* of the birds.

In this happy, peaceful place, I realize the most amazing thing.

My gloomy thoughts aren't the boss of me. I have the power to change how I think.

From that day on, every morning when I wake up and every single night before I go to sleep, I take three slow, deep breaths and think of all the things I'm grateful for.

By the time my ankle is strong enough
to play tennis, so is my mind.

My coach says I'm ready to enter
a tournament.

At home, I picture myself
winning each match, holding
the trophy high.

On the day of the tournament, I wake up slowly
and take three slow, deep breaths. I picture:

My parents

Coco

A beautiful round, fuzzy ball.

My first matches go well. I win easily.
But when I face a super-skilled player in my final match,
I fall apart.

I miss a couple of easy returns.
My serves are a disaster.
I'm getting clobbered!

Argh! I'm so tired.
I'll never win. I should just quit now.

Then I see Coco in the crowd.

I breathe in through my nose:
1, 2, 3, 4.
Then I hold my breath in:
1, 2, 3, 4.

I breathe out through my nose:
1, 2, 3, 4.
Then I hold my breath outside:
1, 2, 3, 4.

I'm back in my zone. Strong and powerful.

I forget about the other player.
It's just me and the fuzzy ball.

I focus on the things I can control:
my stance, my grip, my follow-through.

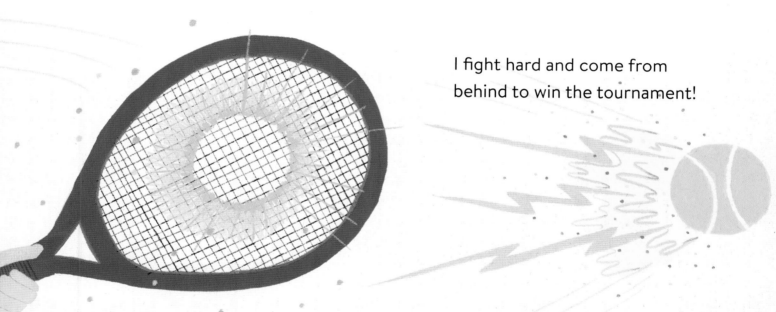

I fight hard and come from behind to win the tournament!

Not every game I play has such a happy ending.
I still lose plenty. But at that match, something
changed for me.

I found the magic hidden in my mind.

Now every morning, I picture myself
strong and powerful on the court.
Just me and the fuzzy ball.

And every single morning,
Mom and Dad and Coco cheer me on.

1

Photo by Kristin Muller

2

3

Photo by Elsa/Getty Images

My family always cheers me on.

## AUTHOR'S NOTE

Like Bibi, I was an active kid with very big dreams. And like Bibi's, my family has been there every step of the way cheering me on.

My parents signed me up for tennis lessons when I was seven years old. When I held the racquet in my hand for the first time, something just clicked. I've loved tennis ever since.

Even though there's nothing I'd rather do than play tennis, it hasn't always been easy. I've had to work hard and sacrifice a lot along the way. I didn't get to do many of the fun things my friends and classmates did. Sometimes it was really hard being so different, and I felt a lot of pressure on and off the court. I've had to overcome injuries. There were times when I would get really down and I'd yell at myself during matches and even practice. All those negative thoughts were hurting me and my game. I knew I had to change how I was thinking.

Everyone who I compete against is a great tennis player. I believe my mental strength helps me win matches. I try to stay focused, be positive and believe in myself.

I've been very lucky to experience things that I dreamed of for so long, like winning the US Open. Work hard for your dreams too. Be persistent. Believe there are good times ahead. It will make you stronger. I'm really, really glad I never gave up on my dreams. Don't give up on yours!

1. My first tennis tournament!

2. Playing in a national tournament when I was 14 years old.

3. Holding the trophy high after I won the 2019 US Open. My dream came true!

Photo by Radka Leitmeritz

# MY MEDITATION ROUTINE

My mom got me into meditation, mindfulness and creative visualization. I've been working on my mental strength for many years now. When I was a little girl, I imagined myself playing in the US Open against Kim Clijsters. Now I picture myself in a match against Serena Williams, dealing with tough situations so when it's time for the real game, I'm prepared for anything that comes my way. I try not to think about who is on the other side of the net. I concentrate on the things that I can control and what I can do to improve. Paying attention to my breathing also helps me stay in the present moment and block out distractions. You can meditate too! You only need about five minutes. Follow these steps:

1. Find a quiet place where you can sit in a comfortable position, either in a chair or on a flat surface. Take a moment to close your eyes and relax.

2. Take a slow, deep breath through your nose. Fill your lungs with air. Slowly let breath out through your mouth. Take a few more deep breaths this way.

3. Try a gratitude mantra. A mantra can be a short sentence, a word or even just a sound that you repeat out loud or in your mind. It will help you focus and feel calm. Let's try this simple mantra: *I am grateful for* _____ . All you need to do is fill in the blank with something that you're thankful for in your life. For me, it's my parents, Coco and a fuzzy tennis ball. Repeat this mantra 10 times. Each time, try to come up with something different that you're grateful for. If you're having trouble coming up with ideas, start small, focusing on things that are close by. Make sure to picture the thing that you're thankful for in your head and feel its good energy.

Me and my mother with Coco when she was just a puppy!

For my parents (and Coco!).
And for everyone working hard to
achieve their dreams. – B.A.

For Pepper, Roxie and all
the other pets out there. – C.O.

For Aria and all the other kids who
live life in motion. – M.B.L.

Tundra Books, an imprint of Penguin Random House Canada Young Readers, a division of Penguin Random House of Canada Limited

Library and Archives Canada Cataloguing in Publication

Title: Bibi's got game : a story about tennis, meditation and a dog named Coco / Bianca Andreescu ; Chelsea O'Byrne.
Names: Andreescu, Bianca, author. | O'Byrne, Chelsea, illustrator.
Identifiers: Canadiana (print) 20210152834 | Canadiana (ebook) 20210152885 | ISBN 9780735270558 (hardcover) | ISBN 9780735270565 (EPUB)
Subjects: LCSH: Meditation–Juvenile literature. | LCSH: Mindfulness (Psychology)–Juvenile literature. | LCSH: Andreescu, Bianca–Juvenile literature. | LCGFT: Picture books. Classification: LCC BF637.M4 A53 2022 | DDC j158.1/2–dc23

Published simultaneously in the United States of America by Tundra Books of Northern New York, an imprint of Penguin Random House Canada Young Readers, a division of Penguin Random House of Canada Limited

Library of Congress Control Number: 2021933734

Unless otherwise credited, all photos courtesy the Andreescu family.

Written with Mary Beth Leatherdale
Edited by Elizabeth Kribs
Designed by Terri Nimmo
The illustrations in this book were made with a combination of gouache, colored pencil and digital tools.
The text was set in Brandon.

Printed in China

www.penguinrandomhouse.ca

1   2   3   4   5      26   25   24   23   22

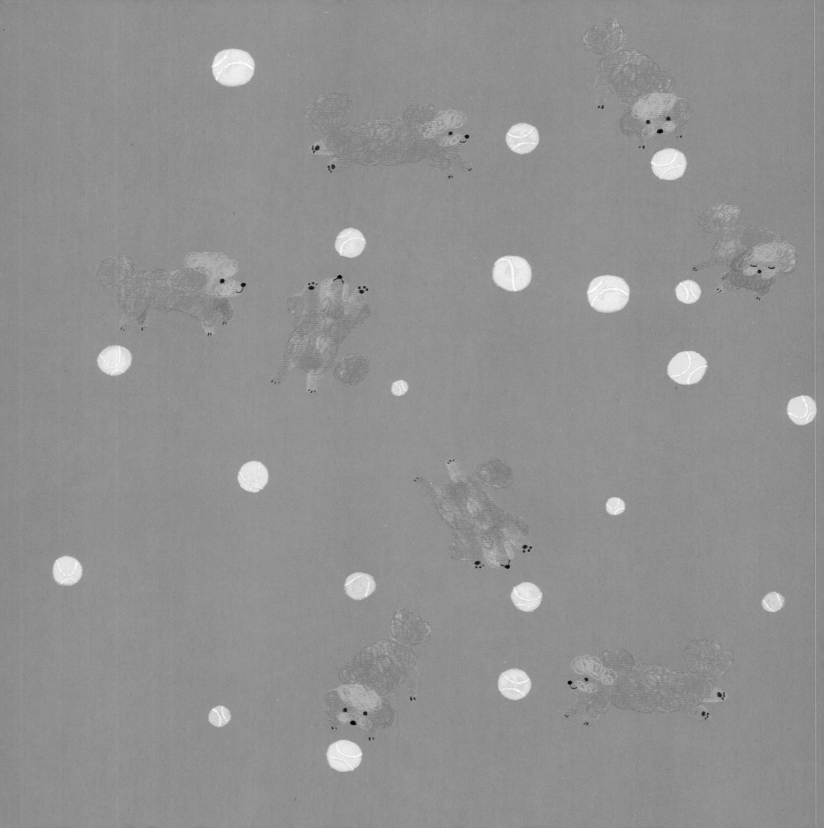